Thanks to my niece, Katie Clark, for the title which started it all,
to Karen Vik Eustis, for our mailbox critiques,
. . . and to Elizabeth Hollow, Joann Johansen Burch,
Kristine O'Connell George, Marion Rosen, and Barney Saltzberg, who
all helped find *Grandma*.
—A.H.W.

To my dear sister,
Lyra Halprin:
encourager,
guide,
friend...
who has taught me about kin
and about the larger issues
and how these *are* the larger issues.
With love.
— A.H.W.

To Grandma
— G. B.

"The Chickadilla Song" arranged by April Halprin Wayland.

Based on *Reuben and Rachel*. Composed by W. Harry Birch and M. William Gooch, 1871.

THIS IS A BORZOI BOOK PUBLISHED BY ALFRED A. KNOPF, INC.

Published in the United States of America by Alfred A. Knopf, Inc., New York, and simultaneously in Canada
by Random House of Canada Limited, Toronto. Distributed by Random House, Inc., New York.

Book design by Mina Greenstein. Manufactured in the United States of America. 10 9 8 7 6 5 4 3 2 1

Library of Congress Cataloging-in-Publication Data

Wayland, April Halprin. It's not my turn to look for Grandma! / by April Halprin Wayland ;

illustrated by George Booth. p. cm. Summary: Grandma is too busy for various family activities until

she's invited to put together a banjo band to entertain them. ISBN 0-679-84491-0 (trade) ISBN 0-679-94491-5 (lib. bdg.)

[1. Grandmothers—Fiction. 2. Family life—Fiction. 3. Music—Fiction.] I. Booth, George, ill. II. Title.

PZ7.W35126It 1995 [E]—dc20 93-7018

It's Not My Turn to Look for Grandma!

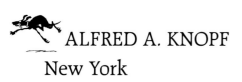

by April Halprin Wayland

illustrated by George Booth

ALFRED A. KNOPF
New York

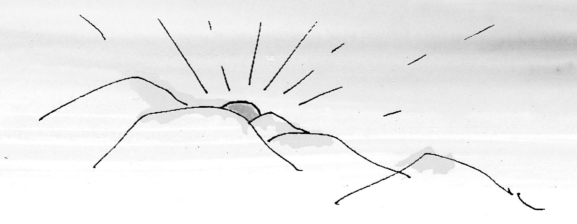

Dawn was just cracking over the hills. Ma was splitting kindling on the back porch.

"Woolie!" she called out. "Where in the hickory stick is Grandma?"

"Dunno," said Woolie. "It's not *my* turn to look for Grandma!"

It was Mack's turn.

"*Maaa-ack!*" called Ma, and sent him a-lookin'. Mack looked and he looked and he sure did look, and, well, friends and neighbors, he finally found Grandma and her dirty old dog telling jokes and soaking their bones in the stewaot on the kitchen stove.

"Grandma!" said Mack, out of breath. "Come tell us stories while we split kindling."

"Tell tales?" said Grandma. "Too busy."

So Mack leaned in and listened hard. Then he ran back and told a tall tale of his own to Woolie and Ma as the wood chips flew.

Noon was sizzling like an egg in a cast-iron pan.
Ma was whacking weeds in the garden. "Woolie,"
she said, "where in turnip tarnation is Grandma?"

"Dunno," said Woolie. "It's not *my* turn to look
for Grandma."

It was Oleanna's turn.

"*Oooleannnnnnna!*" called Ma, and sent her a-lookin'. Oleanna looked and she looked and she sure did look, and, well, friends and neighbors, she finally found Grandma, her dirty old dog, and all of her ducks in the closet, painting the coats new colors.

"Grandma!" said Oleanna, peering in. "Come paint our portrait for posterity."

"Paint a picture?" said Grandma. "Too busy."

So Oleanna opened her eyes wide and watched the colors fly. Then she ran back and painted a picture of Mack and Woolie and Ma watering the peas and the pumpkins.

Afternoon clouds scrambled in the sky. Ma was hammering on the roof.

"Woolie," she pounded, "where in the no-good nails is Grandma?"

"Dunno," said Woolie. "It's not *my* turn to look for Grandma!"

It was Monroe's turn.

"*Monrooooe!*" called Ma, and sent him a-lookin'. Monroe looked and looked and he sure did look, and, well, friends and neighbors, he finally found Grandma, her dirty old dog, all of her ducks, and those nasty porcupines sliding down the haystack two by two.

"Grandma," said Monroe, shading his eyes, "come test the roof with one of your jigs."

"Do a dance?" said Grandma. "Too busy."

So Monroe figured out what to do. He copied the twist Grandma turned each time she reached the haystack bottom and added two do-si-dos of his own. Then he climbed the roof and danced across the shingles while Oleanna and Mack and Woolie and Ma followed behind him patching up the holes.

Shadows were eating up the day. Ma was tuning her fiddle in the yard.

"Woolie," she said, "where in the Talladega two-step is Grandma? And there ain't nobody left, Woolie, so don't you be a-tellin' me it's not *your* turn."

"Yes'm," he said. Then he looked and he looked and he sure did look and, well, friends and neighbors, he finally found Grandma, her dirty old dog, all of her ducks, those nasty porcupines, a raccoon, and a possum sitting around the table playing nine-card stump.

"Grandma," whispered Woolie, peeking at her cards, "play that four of hearts. And we need you and your banjo band."

Grandma slammed down her cards. All the animals stopped their jabbering. It was quiet as a mosquito on skis.

"Never too busy for a banjo band," she said.
Grandma got out her banjo on the spot and invited
all the animals to join her. Ma and the kids put on those
freshly painted coats, and didn't they look grand?

Then Woolie said, "Let's sing the Chickadilla Song!"
So they did, and it went like this:

I lift my shovel, Chick, early in the day,
Cover those middles with new-mown hay,
Feed the chicks and hear them a-squawkin',
A possum in the grain bag and everyone's a-talkin'.

Chickadilla, chickadilla, tickle on the riprap.
Chickadilla, chickadilla, scratching at the gate.
Chickadilla, chickadilla, scatter, scoot, skit-scat!
Sun's coming up, Chick, you're making me late!

I hack away the weeds in the black-eyed peas,
Whitewash the trunks of the walnut trees,
Take a drink of water from the hose by the oak,
Then run to the river for a hound dog soak.

Chickadilla, chickadilla, tickle on the riprap.
Chickadilla, chickadilla, feather on the wing.
Chickadilla, chickadilla, scatter, scoot, skit-scat!
Sun's going down, Chick, it's time for a sing!

And Grandma and her kin
kept hollering out songs until their hollering brought on the night.

Just like it always did.